A VISIT TO CHINA

Story by Mary Packard
Illustrated by Benrei Huang

A Golden Book • New York
Western Publishing Company, Inc. Racine, Wisconsin 53404

 Developed by Nancy Hall, Inc. Library of Congress Catalog Card Number: 90-85682. ISBN: 0-307-12633-1
ISBN: 0-307-62633-4 (lib. bdg.)
A MCMXCI

Su-Lan Wu, who is seven years old, lives in the People's Republic of China. The name of her town is Suzhou. It is small but not very far from Shanghai, China's largest city and seaport.

Su-Lan's father is a sea captain, whose ship is out to sea. Her mother is an artist. When her parents are at work, Su-Lan's grandmother takes care of her.

It is Little New Year, the time when everyone prepares for New Year, China's biggest holiday. There is lots to do, and a happy feeling fills the air as Su-Lan and her family get ready to celebrate.

老方魚鋪
茶

Su-Lan and her grandmother have gone to the market to buy special holiday foods. The color red is everywhere, because in China red is the color of good luck and happiness.

"It is time to say good-bye to the old year and get ready for the new," said Grandma Wu, smiling.

"Things won't be the same this year without Father," Su-Lan said sadly. "This is the first time he won't be home with us for the New Year's celebration. Father is going to miss out on all the fun!"

"I have an idea," said Grandma. "Why don't we buy a diary? Then you can write down everything that happens during the holidays."

"That's a wonderful idea!" exclaimed Su-Lan. "I'll write in it each day, and I won't leave out anything. Then we can share the New Year's celebration with Father when he returns!"

Grandma bought the diary while Su-Lan looked at some of the things in the store.

Su-Lan stopped to admire a poster that showed a woman wearing a lovely strand of pearls. Su-Lan's mother and grandmother owned pearls like them. Her father had brought the pearls home, and Su-Lan knew they would wear them for New Year's and the Lantern Festival.

Su-Lan really loved the Lantern Festival, which is a special celebration when Chinese people welcome the first full moon of the year. Su-Lan wished that she had pearls to wear, too, so that when she got dressed she would feel grown-up—just like her mother and grandmother.

On the way home Su-Lan stopped at her mother's art workshop to show her the diary.

"What a lovely idea!" exclaimed Mrs. Wu. "Father will be so pleased."

The next day Su-Lan got up very early to help her grandmother.

"Little New Year brings many extra chores," said Grandma Wu. "*Zào Shén*, the kitchen god, will not bring good luck in the coming year if everything is not gleaming," she added with a wink.

Finally it was New Year's Eve! While Grandmother prepared the meal, Su-Lan and her mother went to the bakery to buy a special New Year's cake called *Nián Gao*. Then they hung up the good-luck scrolls. In the living room Mother hung one that said "Long Life." On the front door Su-Lan hung another that said "Luck Has Arrived."

When the house was finally ready, Su-Lan took a deep breath. The air was perfumed with lovely smells coming from the kitchen. Su-Lan's heart was filled with joy, and the holiday had not even begun! Su-Lan put on a new dress her mother had made for her.

At midnight, Su-Lan heard the explosions of firecrackers. The New Year's celebration had begun!

The next day Grandma made a big pot of dumplings. She served them to Su-Lan and her mother.

"Whoever bites a dumpling and finds the candy prize is sure to have good luck this year," said Grandma Wu.

Su-Lan bit into dumpling after dumpling.

"I got the prize!" she cried. "I know my wish will come true!"

On the third day of the New Year, everyone gathered outside to watch the "lions" and "dragons" dance through the streets.

"Look how many legs the dragon has!" Su-Lan cried in delight.

"That's so he can carry lots of good luck to us in the New Year," said Grandma Wu.

"How scary the lion looks!" shivered Su-Lan.

"That's so he can scare the old year away," Grandma told her.

Each night Su-Lan wrote about every wonderful thing that happened to her. She could hardly wait to share the diary with her father.

On the fifth day of the New Year everything returned to normal. Su-Lan was feeling grouchy.

"Why do our celebrations have to end, Grandma?" she asked.

"To make room for the new ones," replied Grandma Wu with a chuckle. "Have you forgotten that the Lantern Festival is only ten days away?"

That night Su-Lan's mother took the lanterns out of storage. Together they cleaned them and got them ready for the holiday.

Soon it was time to hang the lanterns. The first day of the full moon had arrived! Grandma came out of the kitchen carrying boxes of special treats from the bakery.

"You may help me stack the cakes," said Grandma Wu.

From time to time, Su-Lan would pop a cake into her mouth. It was easy to see why this was her favorite job!

In the evening Su-Lan, her mother, and grandmother went outside to greet the moon.

Later they all sat down to a scrumptious dinner. But before she could take her first bite, Su-Lan heard a noise at the door.

"It's Father!" she cried, throwing herself into his arms.

Captain Wu explained that his ship needed repairs, so he was forced to bring it back into port. "I see I have arrived just in time," he added, eyeing the feast on the table.

"But first," said Su-lan, "I have a present for you." She ran to get the diary for her father.

"And I have a surprise for you, too," said Captain Wu.

Su-Lan opened the box. Inside was a single, perfect pearl.

"You are becoming quite a young lady," said Su-Lan's father. "I think it is time you have a pearl of your own."

Su-Lan was sure this was going to be the best year ever!

Facts About China

- There are more people (1,013,900,000) in China than in any other country in the world.
- Beijing, with 9 million people, is the capital of China, although Shanghai has a larger population of 12 million.
- When eating with chopsticks, it is considered bad manners to talk, point, or wave them.
- Chinese children go to school six days a week. Because of overcrowding, one group starts at seven-thirty in the morning. They leave at twelve noon, and a second group comes in from one to five in the afternoon. Twice a day the whole school takes a break to do eye and other physical exercises.
- Children in China like to play hopscotch, marbles, Ping-Pong, cat's cradle, and to skip rope. Five stones, another favorite game, is played like jacks.
- The Chinese were the first to discover that silk could be made from the cocoons of silkworms. Other discoveries from China include: kites, the compass, paper, tea, fireworks, printing, ink, clocks, and the wheelbarrow.
- No matter when they were born, all Chinese add a year to their ages on New Year's Day. They also celebrate the actual day of their birth.